T5-AQQ-334

Love,

Bobbie

Christmas, 1988

Christmas
1940

Christmas 1940

by Eleanor Roosevelt

with a Foreword
by Elliott Roosevelt

ST. MARTIN'S PRESS
New York

Christmas 1940.
Copyright © 1940 by Liberty Library Inc.
All rights reserved.
Printed in the United States of America.
No part of this book may be used or reproduced
in any manner whatsoever without written permission
except in the case of
brief quotations embodied in
critical articles or reviews.
For information, address St. Martin's Press,
175 Fifth Avenue, New York, N.Y. 10010.

Library of Congress Cataloging in Publication Data

Roosevelt, Eleanor, 1884-1962.

    Christmas 1940.

    1. Christmas stories.   2. World War, 1939-1945—
Fiction.   I. Title.
PS3535.05487C4   1986   813'.52   86-15456
ISBN 0-312-13401-0

"Christmas 1940" was first published as a short story in
Liberty Magazine.

First U.S. Edition

10 9 8 7 6 5 4 3 2 1

Christmas
1940

Foreword

When my mother wrote this story, for the 1940 Christmas-week edition of *Liberty* magazine, she was deeply concerned for the state of the world. Remember what we faced then—

—Hitler's armies had overrun most of Europe: France, The Netherlands, Belgium, Luxembourg, Norway,

Denmark, Poland, Austria, and Czechoslovakia. Greece, Albania, Yugoslavia, Hungary, and Romania were threatened and would soon fall.

—Britain, holding out alone, had been badly hurt by incessant air attacks. Wolf packs of German submarines hunted the sea lanes that were essential to British survival.

—The Nazi invasion of Russia was still more than six months away. In the winter of 1940, the powerful Soviet

Union remained Hitler's partner in aggression.

—Militarist Japan occupied much of China, and the final defeat of China seemed imminent.

Indeed, it seemed that winter that destruction of civilization and the final enslavement of all mankind was within the reach of the Nazi and Communist and militarist dictatorships. On November 5, 1940 my father was elected to his third term as President of the United

States, and much of the responsibility for preventing the enslavement of the world rested on his shoulders. Naturally, because my mother worked so closely with him, some of it rested on hers, too.

My mother was afraid. Many people were. We feared for humanity. What was more, many families had something very personal to fear: that their sons would have to fight on the battlefields of a war that had already proved terribly costly in human life. I was then serving in the armed forces, and my mother knew that my brothers would have to serve too, when war came.

Though fear gripped Eleanor Roosevelt that winter, she was sustained by her faith: by her religious faith, yes, but also by her confidence in human kind.

All her life my mother lived by her principles. I have known almost no one who could draw strength the way she did from her confident belief that some truths cannot be overcome by lies, that mankind will ultimately fight off every oppression, and that somehow we will achieve our Creator's purpose for us.

My mother believed that a Supreme Being created all of us, that He watches over us, and that through His power we will in the end live free. She believed it was God's purpose that we should love and help our neighbors—an element of her faith that her own life exemplified with rare beauty.

She tried to express some of this in the little Christmas story you are about to read.

* * *

I was not living with my parents when Mother wrote this story. I was serving in the Army Air Corps. I did not see her at work on it, but these are some of the things that were happening at the time when she wrote—

—On October 28, Italy invaded Greece.

— On the night of November 14, more than five hundred German planes bombed Coventry, killing and injuring more than one thousand people, and destroying much of the city, including its splendid Gothic cathedral.

—On the night of November 22, more than eight hundred people were killed in an air raid on Birmingham.

— On November 26 the Nazis began to herd Polish Jews into the Warsaw ghetto.

Obviously, my mother was acutely aware of all these events. She was especially aware of the human suffering they represented.

Her Christmas story is set in the occupied Netherlands, and tells how the simple faith of a small, suffering family sustains itself against the evil force of the oppressor. This faith and a small act of defiance express the essence of my mother's belief.

"Have faith," she was saying to the oppressed peoples of the world. "Have faith and do not despair. God will overcome the powerful and greedy tyrants. Freedom will be yours again."

"Christmas 1940" is the kind of story that is rarely written today. I suppose our tastes have changed, as has our style. I can't help but feel, however, that this little story is, in its own way, timeless. It carries a message that is as valid today as it was in 1940.

In fact, I am sure that if my mother were still living, she would say to the peoples of Eastern Europe and to oppressed peoples everywhere—"Have faith. This too will pass, and all will be free."

ELLIOTT ROOSEVELT
Indian Wells, California
February 26, 1986

St. Nicholas' Eve, 1940, was cold and the snow was falling.

On the hearth in Marta's home there was a fire burning, and she had been hugging that fire all day, asking her mother to tell her stories, telling them afterward to her doll.

This was not like St. Nicholas' Eve
of last year. Then her father had come
home. Seven-year-old Marta asked her
mother to tell her the story over and
over again; so her mother, whose fingers
were never idle now that she was alone
and had to feed and clothe herself and
Marta, sat and knit long woolen stockings and talked of the past which would
never come again, and of St. Nicholas'
Eve, 1939.

The war was going on in Europe in

1939, but Jon was only mobilized. He was just guarding the border, and was allowed to come home for the holiday. Marta's mother said:

"On Monday I got the letter, and on Tuesday, St. Nicholas' Eve, he came. I got up early in the morning and started cleaning the house. I wanted everything to shine while your father was home. Soon I called you, and when you were dressed and had had your breakfast, you took your place in the window, watching for him to come. Every time you saw a speck way down the road, you would call out to me, but I had time to get much of the holiday cooking prepared and the house in good order before you finally cried, 'Here he is!' and a cart stopped by our gate. You threw open the door and you ran down the path. I saw him pick you up in his arms, but he was in such a hurry that he carried you right on in with him and met me as I was running halfway down the path.''

Her mother always sighed and Marta wondered why her eyes looked so bright; then she would go on and tell of Jon's coming into the house and insisting on saying: *"Vroolyk Kerstfeest,"* meaning ''Merry Christmas,'' all over again to her and to Marta, just as though he had not greeted them both outside.

They both felt sorry that the two grandmothers and the two grandfathers

could not come that year. Little Marta
loved to think about her grandfathers.
One grandfather could tell her so much
about the animals and the birds and
make them seem just like people, and
her mother's father could tell her stories, long, long stories, about things that
happened in cities, about processions
and having seen the Queen, and so
many wonderful things that she could
dream about after the visit was over. It
was a disappointment when the grand-

parents could not be with them for this St. Nicholas' Eve.

Little Marta did not know it, but to her father's parents it was more than a disappointment. They had wanted so much to see their son again. Like all mothers, his mother feared the worst where her own boy was concerned. Perhaps she had had a premonition of what the future held, but, as with all peasants, the hard facts of life are there to be counted, and the money saved for the trip would keep food in the larder if the winter was going to be as hard as everything indicated, so they did not travel.

Marta's mother had told her that perhaps St. Nicholas, on his white horse with his black servant, Peter, would not bring any presents that year to fill her wooden shoes, but Marta would not believe it. Her first question to her father was, "Will St. Nicholas forget us?"

"No, little Marta," said her father. "The good saint will come tonight if you go to bed like a good girl and go quickly to sleep.''

Marta put her little shoes down by the big fireplace, and her mother took her into the bedroom and tucked her away behind the curtains which shielded her bunk along the wall on the cold winter night.

On Christmas morning Marta woke and ran to look for her wooden shoes. ''St. Nicholas has been here!'' she cried, ''and he's given me many sweets, a doll, and bright red mittens just like the stockings mother made me as a Christmas gift.''

Then the whole family went skating on the river and there were many other little girls with their fathers and mothers. Every one glided about, and the babies were pushed or dragged in their little sleds. The boys and girls chased one another. Sometimes long lines took hands and, after skating away, gathered in a circle, going faster

and faster until they broke up because
they could not hold on any longer.

*   *   *

Then at last they went home to dinner.
On the table was a fat chicken and a
good soup.

At first they ate silently, and then,
as the edge of their hunger wore off,
they began to talk.

"Marta," said her father, "have
you learned to read in school yet? Can

you count how many days there are in a month?''

''Oh, yes,'' replied Marta, ''and mother makes me mark off every day that you're gone, and when we are together we always say, 'I wonder if father remembers what we are doing now,' and we try to do just the things we do when you are home so you can almost see us all the time.''

Her father smiled rather sadly, and then her mother said:

"Jon, perhaps it is good for us all that we have to be apart for a while, because we appreciate so much more this chance of being together. There is no time for cross words when you know how few minutes there are left. It should make us all realize what it would be like if we lived with the thought of how quickly life runs away before us."

A curious look came into his eyes and Jon thought for a moment with anguish of what he might have to do some day to other homes and other children, or what might happen to his, and then he pulled himself together and you could almost hear him say, ''This at least is going to be a happy memory,'' and turning to Marta, he began to tease her about her fair hair, which stuck out in two little pigtails from the cap which she wore on her head. Seizing one of them, he said:

''I can drive you just like an old horse. I will pull this pigtail and you

will turn this way. I will pull the other
one and you go that way.''

* * *

Such a jolly, happy time, and then, as
the dusk fell, Marta's father put on his
uniform again, kissed her mother, and
hugged Marta tightly, saying, ''Take
good care of *moeder* until I come back.''

Then he was gone and they were
alone again. The year seemed to travel
heavily. First, letters came from Jon,

and then one day a telegram, and her
mother cried and told Marta that her
father would never come back; but
her mother never stopped working, for
now there was no one to look after them
except God, and He was far away in His
heaven. Marta talked to Him sometimes
because mother said He was every one's
Father, but it never seemed quite true.
Marta could believe, however, that the
Christ child in the Virgin's arms in the
painting in the church was a real child

and she often talked to Him.

Strange things Marta told the Christ child. She confided in Him that she never had liked that uniform which her father went away in. It must have had something to do with his staying away. He had never gone away in the clothes he wore every day and not come back. She liked him best in his everyday clothes. She was never afraid of him then, and he had a nice homey smell; something of the cows and horses came into the house with him, and, like a good little country girl, Marta liked that smell. She told the Christ child that her mother had no time to play with her any more. She had to work all the time, and sometimes tears fell on her work and she could not answer Marta's questions.

There was no school any more for her to go to, and on the road she met children who talked a strange language and they made fun of her and said now this country was theirs. It was all very hard to understand and she wondered if the Christ child really did know what was happening to little children down here on earth. Sometimes there was nothing to eat in the house, and then both she and her mother went hungry to bed, and she woke in the morning to find her mother gone and it would be considerably later before her mother returned with something for breakfast.

Thinking of all these things as her

mother told the story again on this St. Nicholas' Eve, 1940, Marta took off her wooden shoes and put them down beside the open fire. Sadly her mother said, "St. Nicholas will not come tonight," and he did not. Marta had an idea of her own, however, which she thought about until Christmas Eve came. Then she said to her mother, "There is one candle left from last year's feast. May I light it in the house so the light will shine out for the Christ child to see His way? Perhaps He will come to us since St. Nicholas forgot us.''

Marta's mother shook her head but smiled, and Marta took out the candle and carefully placed it in a copper candlestick.

Marta wanted to see how far the light would shine out into the night, so she slipped into her wooden shoes again, put her shawl over her head, opened the door, and slipped out into the night. The wind was blowing around her and

she could hardly stand up. She took two
or three steps and looked back at the
window. She could see the twinkling
flame of the candle, and while she stood
watching it, she was conscious of a tall
figure in a dark cloak standing beside
her.

*   *   *

Just at first she hoped the tall figure
might be her father, but he would not
have stood there watching her without

coming out into the candlelight and picking her up and running into the house to greet her mother. She was not exactly afraid of this stranger, for she was a brave little girl, but she felt a sense of chill creeping through her, for there was something awe-inspiring and rather repellent about this personage who simply stood in the gloom watching her.

Finally he spoke.

''What are you doing here, little

girl?''

Very much in awe, Marta responded: ''I came out to make sure that the Christ child's candle would shine out to guide His footsteps to our house.''

''You must not believe in any such legend,'' remonstrated the tall dark man. ''There is no Christ child. That is a story which is told for the weak. It is ridiculous to believe that a little child could lead the people of the world, a foolish idea claiming strength through love and sacrifice. You must grow up and acknowledge only one superior, he who dominates the rest of the world through fear and strength.''

This was not very convincing to Marta. Why, she talked to the Christ child herself! But she had been taught to be respectful and to listen to her elders and so silence reigned while she wondered who this man was who said such strange and curious things. Was he wanted them. That had been hard because they loved their animals and they a bad man? Did he have something to do with her father's going away and not coming back? Or with her mother's worrying so much and working so hard?

He had done her no harm—at least, no bodily harm—and yet down inside her something was hurt. Things could be taken away from people. They had had to give up many of their chickens and cows because the government

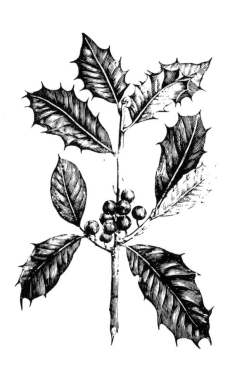

had cared for them, and it meant also
that they would have little to eat and
much less money when they lost them.
But that was different from the way
this man made her feel. He was taking
away a hope, a hope that someone could
do more than even her mother could do,
could perhaps make true the dream,
that story she told herself every night,
both awake and asleep, of the day when
her father would come home; when he
would put her on his shoulder and they

would go skating on the canal. Somehow this man hurt that dream and it was worse than not having St. Nicholas come. It seemed to pull down a curtain over the world.

Marta was beginning to feel very cold and very much afraid, but all her life she had been told to be polite to her elders and ask for permission to do anything she wished to do. She said, ''I am hoping the Christ child will come. May I go in now and will you not come into my house?''

The man seemed to hesitate a minute, but perhaps he decided it would be interesting to see the inside of such a humble home where there was so much simple faith. In any case, he wanted to impress upon this child and upon her mother that foolish legends were not the right preparation for living in a world where he, the power, dominated, so he followed Marta into the house.

Marta's mother, who had been sit-

ting by the fire knitting when Marta
went out, was still there, yes, but in her
arms was a baby and around the baby a
curious light shone, and Marta knew
that the Christ child had come. The man
in the door did not know; he thought it
was an ordinary room with an ordinary
baby in a woman's arms.

Striding in, he said, "Madam, you
have taught this child a foolish legend.
Why is she burning a candle in the hope
that the Christ child will come?"

The woman answered in a very low
voice, ''To those of us who suffer, that
is a hope we may cherish. Under your
power there is fear, and you have created a strength before which people
tremble. But on Christmas Eve strange
things happen and new powers are
sometimes born.''

Marta was not interested any more
in the tall figure with the cloak. The
Christ child was there in her mother's
lap. She could tell Him all her troubles

and He would understand why she prayed above everything else for the return of her father. St. Nicholas would never again leave them without Christmas dinner and she could have a new doll and the sweets which she longed to taste again. Perhaps, if only she went to sleep like a good little girl there would be a miracle and her father would be there. Off she trotted to the second room, and climbed behind the curtain.

Marta could not go to sleep at once

because, there was no sound from the other room, she still could not free herself from the thought of that menacing figure. She wondered if he was responsible for the tears of the little girl up the road whose father had not come home last year and who had not been visited either by St. Nicholas.

Then before her eyes she suddenly saw a vision of the Christ child. He was smiling and seemed to say that the little girl up the road had her father this year and that all was well with her. Marta was happy—fathers are so very nice. Perhaps if she prayed again to the Christ child, when she woke up He would have her father there too, and so she said first the prayer she had always been taught to say and then, just for herself, she added:

"Dear Christ child, I know You will understand that though God is the Father of us all, He is very, very far away and the fathers we have down here are so much closer. Please bring mine back so that we can have the cows, the pigs, and the chickens again and all we want to eat and the tears will not be in my mother's eyes.'' The murmur of her prayer died away as she fell asleep.

A long time the power stood and watched Marta's mother, and finally there came over him a wave of strange feeling. Would any one ever turn eyes on him as lovingly as this woman's eyes turned on that baby? Bowing low before her, he said, ''Madam, I offer you ease and comfort, fine raiment, delicious food. Will you come with me where these things are supplied but where you cannot keep to your beliefs?''

Marta's mother shook her head and looked down at the baby lying in her lap. She said, ''Where you are, there are power and hate and fear of people, one of another. Here there are none of the things you offer, but there is the Christ child. The Christ child taught love. He drove the money-changers out of the temple, to be sure, but that was because He hated the system they represented. He loved His family, the poor, the sinners, and He tried to bring out in each one the love for Him and for each other which would mean a Christlike spirit which makes us live forever. You will go out into the night again, the cold night, to die as all must die who are not born again through Him at Christmastime.''

The man turned and went out, and as he opened the door, he seemed to be engulfed in the dark and troubled world without. The snow was falling and the wind was howling, the sky was gloomy overhead. All that he looked upon was fierce and evil. These evil forces of nature were ruling also in men's hearts and they brought sorrow and misery to many human beings. Greed, personal ambition, and fear all were strong in the world fed by con-

stant hate. In the howling of the wind
he heard these evil spirits about him,
and they seemed to run wild, unleashed.

* * *

This has happened, of course, many
times in the world before, but must it go
on happening forever? Suddenly he
turned to look back at the house from
which he had come. Still from the window shone the little child's candle and
within he could see framed the figure of

the mother and the baby. Perhaps that was a symbol of the one salvation there was in the world, the heart of faith, the one hope of peace. The hope he had taken away from Marta for the moment shone out increasingly into the terrible world, even though it was only the little Christ child's candle.

With a shrug of his shoulders he turned away to return to the luxury of power. He was able to make people suffer. He was able to make people do his will, but his strength was shaken and it always will be. The light in the window must be the dream which holds us all until we ultimately win back to the things for which Jon died and for which Marta and her mother were living.